Frank Howard

Colour As a Means of Art

Frank Howard

Colour As a Means of Art

1st Edition | ISBN: 978-3-75238-603-5

Place of Publication: Frankfurt am Main, Germany

Year of Publication: 2020

Outlook Verlag GmbH, Germany.

COLOUR

AS A

MEANS OF ART

BY FRANK HOWARD

PREFACE.

In the Sketcher's Manual, the general principles of making pictures in black and white, or, as it is technically termed, in Chiaroscuro, have been briefly, but it is hoped distinctly, explained. The following work on Colouring proceeds upon the same method. It treats first of the arrangements of masses of colours which have been established by various masters or schools, and which have been recognized as satisfactory or agreeable by the public voice; it then points out the abstract principles to which these several arrangements may be referred; and finally directs attention to the qualities of Colouring in Art which are requisite as regards the imitation of Nature. It does not profess to descend to details, for these require a considerable advance in the Art, and consequently could not possibly be rendered intelligible in any publication, because they would require the exercise of first-rate powers, to colour every individual impression of the plates. For examples of the details of colouring, the Amateur and the Student must be referred to the best pictures of the several masters whose general principles are herein exhibited. But it should be observed, that although the several masters, whose names have been brought forward in the present work, and in the Sketcher's Manual, as the originators of the several principles of Chiaroscuro and Colour, are generally distinguished by some exercise of the principles to which their names are attached, they have produced many and valuable works in other and very different styles. It is not intended to imply that all the works of these masters are constructed upon the same principles; still less is it intended to imply that the principal merit of these masters resides in the particular principle of picture-making, which they have mainly, if not entirely, contributed to develope; for this would reduce the art of painting to a "mechanical trade," or mere means of gratifying the eye. Least of all has it been intended to afford to critics a means of attack upon the modern masters, whose names have been introduced into these little works, as "painters of pictures on receipt, or on a principle of manufacture." The development of a new principle of Art, whether relating to Composition, Chiaroscuro, or Colour, is as meritorious and worthy of distinction as, if not more so than, the production of an able work upon the principles of Art previously established by others.

The author is fully sensible that *he* must submit to criticism with respect to whatever he may place before the public; nor is he in the least disposed to complain of any censure of the *matter contained* in the works, or of the *manner* in which that matter is placed before the public. He can even afford to smile at the criticism that a work addressed to the Amateur and the Student on Picture-making in Chiaroscuro, "will not make a Raffaelle or a Titian," particularly as the great merit of the latter was colouring; and he may observe that he does not expect that even the present work, which is solely devoted to colouring, "will make a Titian." It will be sufficient if he shall have placed in a tangible shape before the reader *some* of the principles by which the effects of Colouring, and light and shade have been made, by certain masters, subservient to higher purposes;—the Art is but the means to an end. But the author feels that he has a right to complain of a criticism of his work, in which the *censures* of the *critic* upon *third* parties are made to appear to have proceeded from the author; and he now begs to disclaim having said anything disrespectful either of Mr. Stanfield or Mr. Roberts, either directly or indirectly, as will be evident upon the inspection of the Sketcher's Manual.

And the author feels it necessary to remove an erroneous impression with respect to the nature and intention of these works, by stating, that they are expressly intended for the Amateur or the Beginner in Art; that they are not intended to be argumentative or controversial; nor are any matters introduced that require the support of argument, evidence, or authority, although these could easily be adduced, if requisite; but the desire of the author has been to lay before the Amateur such principles of Art as have received the sanction of years, and are universally appreciated by the public in their effects: and the only merit claimed is that of having brought them together in such a form as to distinguish them clearly; and to render the principles as evident as possible. But there is no pretension of limiting the whole Art of Colouring to the principles of Colouring contained herein.

For the method in which the plates of the present work have been executed, I am indebted to a recent improvement in Lithography, made by Mr. Hullmandell. It is capable of producing more nearly the effects of painting than any other style of engraving; but from these plates professing only to represent masses of Colour and general tone, and being the first that have been attempted in this particular application, they are not calculated to display Mr. Hullmandell's improvement to advantage.

INTRODUCTION.

Sir Joshua Reynolds in one of his Discourses has stated, that the Edifice of Art has been gradually raised by the contributions of the great men of past ages, and that although every addition to knowledge required the exertion of a mind far in advance of its contemporaries to effect it, the results have now become the common property of all artists, and may easily be appropriated by every Student—"that much may now be taught, which it required vast genius to discover."

It will not be necessary to adduce any argument in support of this proposition. The difference of opinion will principally refer to "what part can be taught?" And hereon there have been as great divisions and disputes as have arisen with regard to the part of the pig that was forbidden to be eaten by the followers of Mahomet; only it should be observed that the discussions have terminated in an almost opposite result; for whereas the whole pig was eaten, scarcely any of the Art has been taught.

Numerous works have been published and numerous methods of instruction adopted; but they are almost all directed to points of mechanical execution, or the representation of individual objects, which mainly depend upon skill.

Skill is the natural result of practice or fortunate organization, and will, of course, differ with the perseverance or capacity of the student, which has led to the persuasion that the productions of Art are dependent upon what is called natural genius.

But what is *known* of Art may be as easily communicated as any other fact, and as easily acquired as a knowledge of history, or any other appeal to the memory, and is indispensable equally to the critic and to the amateur. On this subject there are few if any works; and it is rarely touched by professed teachers of the Art.

The method of private tuition at present in favour is, to make a drawing before the pupil, who is expected to appreciate the course of proceeding, and to imitate the effect.

Watching a drawing thus in progress, it will be observed that the greater part is done apparently without a thought; it appears to be literally at the "fingers' ends" of the artist: and this will be found to comprehend much, it not all that confers the effect of a picture. But in what does this consist? Repeated practice, and continued study of works of art, will undoubtedly, *in time*, bring it to the "fingers' ends" of the student also, and it will insensibly become an inexplicable habit, manner or style. But this is, in fact, what may be taught or communicated in a short time; it is the knowledge resulting from the experience of ages,—the edifice built up of discoveries from time to time contributed to the fund of Art by the success and failures of our predecessors. This is the *knowledge* or science of painting, which should precede all practice or attainment of skill, and such portion as relates to colouring, it is the intention of the present work to supply. Skill will follow as a result of the endeavour to make use of the means to produce the end—Pictures.

There has been, unfortunately, so great confusion in the use of the terms applicable to Colours, that it becomes difficult to convey any distinct information respecting them, without hazarding the charge of pedantry by limiting the signification of certain words. Tints, Tones, and Shades of Colour have been, and still are, too commonly used so indiscriminately to mean the same and different things, that no definite impression can be given, unless there exist a previous knowledge of the mode in which each word is applied. It will, therefore, be necessary to explain the meanings with which each word will be used in the present work.

TINTS are those specific and definite qualities of colours, by which the individuals of a class are distinguished from each other: as of Reds; Scarlet, Crimson, Pink, Rose-colour, &c.: of Greens; Apple-green, Olive-green, Pea-green, &c.: of Yellows; Straw-colour, Amber, &c.: of Blues; Sky-blue, Garter-blue, Indigo, &c.

SHADES OF COLOUR imply the degree of brilliancy or depth, as bright or deep Crimson; light or dark Blue.

TONES OF COLOUR are of more general application, as indicating the general aspect of classes of Tints or Shades; and especially designating the degree of warmth or coldness: as cool greens, warm greys. There may be lighter and darker *Shades* of the same TONE, but not of the same TINT. Rose-colour and Crimson may be said to be lighter and darker shades of the same *Tone*.

The word Tone is also used by itself in opposition to crudity or rawness of colour; and hence is technically descriptive of the ternary compounds, of whatever tint or shade; while the primary colours and the binary compounds, Blue, Red and Yellow, and Purple, Orange and Green, are technically distinguished as Colour. The lighter shades of Tone in this sense are technically included under the term *Greys*; warm, as they contain Orange;

6

cool, as they contain Purple or Green. Tints and Tones are further classed as *pure*, as they approach purple, and those tints observed in Mother of Pearl, hence, also pearly tints; warm or hot as they approach Orange; heavy, and unless they are exceedingly transparent, muddy, as they approach Green.

HALF-TINTS express those gradations of *colour*, and HALF-LIGHTS those gradations of *light*, between the greatest brilliancy and the shadows.

Colours are said to be SUPPORTED by others which present some resemblance, but are inferior in brilliancy; as blues by purples, crimsons by reddish-browns, yellows by orange:

—CONTRASTED by those which are the most opposite, as blues by orange or browns, reds by green, yellows by purples:

—BALANCED when by opposition they are so neutralized that no one appears principal or predominant.

The author of a recent publication on Colour is quite in error, when, in describing technical terms, he states "the Balance of Colouring is the harmony produced by *supporting* one colour by *another* introduced in *different parts* of the picture, either *of the same colour*, or one approaching to it." This is SPREADING *a colour* THROUGH the picture, and though it may *contribute* to the balance of colouring by *contrasting* and *neutralizing* the *other* colours in the work, it is in itself the very opposite of the *balance* of *colouring*, as it consists entirely in loading one side of the beam. To this it may be added that colours are said to be SUPPORTED by similar tints *adjacent*, and ECHOED by them when "in different parts of the picture."

There are many other errors in the book above-mentioned, but as this is not intended to be a controversial disquisition, those mistakes only will be noticed which might otherwise lead to confusion; but to the correction.

The definition of "MELLOWNESS," as "caused by those warm colours which, when blended, produce an agreeable *tone* or *hue*, and would then be said to *sympathize* and create *harmony*," is as incorrect and indefinite, as the remainder of the paragraph is without foundation:—"On the contrary, if, in mixing two or more colours, a disagreeable and harsh effect were produced, they would be said to have an *antipathy*, and create *rawness*—this adulteration of one colour by another causes what painters term a MUDDY effect." Painters term an effect *muddy* when it is dirty in colour and wanting in transparency. This fancy respecting the sympathy and antipathy of certain

7

colours, which is more distinctly alluded to in the following passage:
—"when, to produce a particular tint, the mixing of two colours which do not sympathize is unavoidable; one or more may be introduced whose sympathy is greater, that a pleasing and harmonious effect may be produced, &c."—this is wholly groundless. How the sympathy and antipathy alluded to are supposed to act is not very evident, but they have no existence whatever.

The definition of a "PEARLY HUE," as "obtained by softening or blending the *warm* colours without adulterating one with the other," is equally liable to objection as untrue.

The attempt at a philosophical account of the *cause* of the colours produced at sunset and sunrise, has been incidentally exposed in the third chapter of the present work. This error undoubtedly does not originate with the professed author of the publication alluded to; and as the greater part of the book is evidently, though without acknowledgment, compiled from Mr. Burnett and other writers on the subject, the other errors are probably in a great measure also the result of compilation.

CHAPTER I.

COLOURING AS A MEANS OF ART.

Colouring is the decorative part of Art. It answers to Rhythm and Rhyme in poetry, as the means of attracting the senses. As it is a means of producing, so its indispensable qualification is,—BEAUTY. In the higher aims of Art it should be made subservient to Character and Expression, by according with the nature of the subject; but, still under the limitation and regulation of those principles which govern Pictorial Effect. Under all circumstances, and to whatsoever purposes applied, the first qualification of Colouring as a means of Art is, that it should produce a Picture.

A picture has been elsewhere defined as an arrangement of one or more objects and accessories so as to afford an agreeable subject of Contemplation. And the principles which regulate Chiaroscuro and general arrangement for this purpose, have been pointed out. The same principles must regulate Colouring as a means of Art.

The mere representation of any object, however accurately detailed and coloured, does not constitute a picture. It must be represented with accessories and under Pictorial Effect. This as regards Chiaroscuro has been shown to depend upon Breadth. As regards Colouring it depends upon Harmony.

CHAPTER I.

SECTION I.

HARMONY.

Harmony is a term borrowed from the sister Art of Music, to denote a degree of relation or congruity between two or more colours, so as mutually to support or develope each other's beauties, as is the case with a chord or concord of sounds. The degrees of relation, or qualification for harmony, of sounds, can be ascertained by mathematical calculation incapable of erroneous results. Not so, those of Colours; at least in the present state of the science of Optics. If it should be proved that colours are the effect of vibrations of the air, or any other fluid, as are sounds, the Harmony of Colours may equally become the subject of mathematical calculation, with equally certain results; at present we cannot go beyond rude approximations by guess or supposition; and are vaguely placed under the regulation of *Taste*,

9

itself as Protean and undefined.

The theory of the three or seven colours being all equally necessary to each other, which has been derived from the division of the ray of light by a prism, has been supposed to afford the relative proportions of the various tints necessary to Harmony in a picture, *because existing in light*; and fanciful, but entirely unfounded, analogies have been drawn by enthusiasts between the seven colours and the seven notes, and the three colours and the notes of the common chord in music: but without going into the question of how far this would be likely to assist in our present inquiry, *if true*, it may be sufficient to observe that these relative proportions *vary* with the substance of the prism by means of which the ray of light is divided; so that the whole induction falls to the ground.

But were the proportions always the same, the induction would be equally untenable. For, though light may be very beautiful; and the Rainbow may be very beautiful; a totally different kind of beauty is required for a picture. The colours of the Rainbow may perfectly harmonize; but it is more than doubtful whether the person whose whole picture was a representation of a Rainbow, would be considered to have produced a finely coloured work of Art.

Harmony, in Pictorial Colour, does not depend upon any particular proportionate quantities of the different tints; nor in any particular disposition or arrangement of them; but upon the qualities and the treatment of the individual colours. A picture may be painted with every variety of the most brilliant colours; or, on the other hand, as Rembrandt treated light, the work may contain only one small spark of colour, the remainder being made up of neutral tints; and even the small spark of colour may be dispensed with, and the whole picture be made up of a variety of tones.

Having dwelt so much in the Sketcher's Manual, upon the principle of Breadth being indispensable for the production of Pictorial Effect, it will scarcely be requisite to point out that it is equally necessary that Colours should be so treated as to produce *Unity*; and that, as with lights and shadows, so whatever variety of tints may be introduced into a picture, they must be so blended and incorporated with each other, that they still form parts of a whole;—that whether the lights be white, and the shadows black, or differently coloured, the same necessity for graduation remains; so that Colours must not be in flat patches. And in the treatment of Colours, besides the graduation requisite for Breadth of Chiaroscuro, it is necessary to pay attention to the peculiar quality termed TONE, which is indispensable in a coloured Work of Art.

As well as Breadth of Chiaroscuro, there must be BREADTH OF TONE, the fundamental quality of Harmony.

CHAPTER I.

SECTION II.

TONE.

This is a term also borrowed from the vocabulary of Music, to denote a property or quality of Colour, the opposite of gaudiness or harshness; and implies a richness or sobriety, inviting quiet contemplation. It confers what is technically termed *repose*. It bears that relation to colours in general, that the quality of a musical note does to that of an unmusical sound or mere noise. In Music, this is known to depend upon the vibrations of the air being *isochronous*, or at regular intervals. Should it be discovered that Colours are also produced by vibrations, Tone in its present application may prove to arise from a similar regularity.

Tone implies a degree of transparency, which in Oil colours is attainable with great facility, by a process termed *glazing*; viz. passing a transparent colour over a previously prepared tint. There are also some other practical methods of producing it, which are more advisable in certain cases, but which need not be further noticed here. In Water colours, the greater number of pigments used are transparent, and the legitimate method of using them proceeds upon the principle of working entirely in transparent media; which has, at all times, excited great hopes with regard to that branch of Art, as affording a better means than Oil colours (in which the light tints are all composed with opaque white) of producing the brilliancy and truth of Nature, in combination with the transparency (tone) which is required in a work of Art. And it is to be regretted, that in some few, and those popular instances, this advantage arising out of the legitimate use of Water colours, should have been thrown away, without obtaining any equivalent, other than that of hiding or correcting blunders; and that attempts should have been made, by the use of opaque body colours, and a similar method of working, to imitate the effect of Oil painting. The progress of the true art of Water-colour drawing, must necessarily receive a check from the adoption of such a practice, which will doubtless be sanctioned by the idle or the hurried; and attempts to carry out the original prospects and genuine advantages of the transparent medium, will probably become rare, if they should not cease entirely.

It is true that opaque Water-colours are supposed to have an advantage over Oil-colours, in light and brilliant parts, in consequence of the tendency of the Oil (the *vehicle*, as it is technically termed) to come to the surface, and thus to give a tinge to, or obscure, the purer tints of skies and distant brilliant objects. On this account, they are said to be used by Turner in these parts, when he desires to attain great clearness and purity of colour. But, however, the *union* of Water-colours with Oil may be advantageous for these purposes, and thus *Opaque* Water-colours may receive a partial sanction; it cannot be denied that, in the instances previously alluded to, in which the Opaque Water-colours are used for no other purpose than the facility of recovering half-tints that had been too much obscured, the only advantage of Water-colours is abandoned, without obtaining the equivalent of *richness*, arising from texture in Oil; and the purity of the one art is lost, without attaining the force of the other. A crumbly, bungling appearance is produced, and for no reason, as the practice can never be successfully employed in the parts or objects, in which the use of semi-transparent colours is so invaluable in Oil. And in fact, Opacity, the reverse of what is desired, Tone, is produced by the very same means in Water-colours, by which transparency is attained in Oil.

Breadth of Tone is obtained by a process termed *breaking the colours*, which is the same with the method of incorporating lights with each other, described in the Sketcher's Manual; viz. graduating each tint into those adjacent, by which means a certain degree of affinity is diffused throughout the whole picture, and Harmony, or Breadth of Tone, is produced. The same results are effected, by a process perhaps abused in the present day, termed Glazing, which consists in passing some transparent pigment of the tone desired, over the whole picture, and thus breaking all the tints in the work with the same colour which produces the affinity required.

CHAPTER II.

RULES FOR PRODUCING PICTURES IN COLOUR.

Although Harmony or Pictorial Colouring does not *depend* upon any *particular* quantities or arrangement of *particular* tints, as the slightest consideration of the infinite variety of Pictures that have been produced will prove; certain quantities and arrangements of certain colours, have been found to effect it.

These discoveries have been made from time to time, and have each been adopted as principles by different artists; and though admitting of considerable variation in details, their effects have been so evidently distinguished by the public as uniform in general aspect, that they have been ranged in classes or schools, to one of which any individual work is instantly referred, by those who have even a slight acquaintance with the Art.

By *writers* upon Art it has been very generally contended, that there *must* be a balance of warm and cold colours. A little consideration will show, that this, as well as *all* restrictive regulations, such as that blue must not come in the front of the picture, &c. are unfounded, or nearly the whole of the Dutch school of landscape and interiors must be condemned as wanting in Harmony, or bad colourists; for Ruysdael and Hobbima, Teniers and Ostade, seem to have had a horror of warm colours, while, on the other hand, Cuyp and Both seem to have had an equal dread of cool tints. That a balance of warm and cold colour is *one* principle by which Pictorial Harmony may be obtained, is perfectly true; and that there are various means of balancing them is also true; which affords numerous varieties of style or character of pictures. And that the principle deduced by Sir Joshua Reynolds from the Venetian school, that one-third of the picture should (may) be cool, and the remaining two-thirds warm, is also just; and will be productive of beautiful results. The error consists in making these relative proportions *indispensable* to Harmony.

This chapter will contain such principles as have been found to ensure Harmony. There may, perhaps, be many others in store for future discovery.

These principles are of universal application, whatever objects may be the subject of the drawing or picture, whether landscape, figures, animals, flowers, or altogether; and they are wholly independent of Poetical or Dramatic colouring,—the application of colour to Expression and Character, —and of the colouring of individual objects.

The art of composition, in regard to colour, consists in arranging objects in such a manner, that their true colouring will produce the combination required by the principle adopted. The art of too many of the artists of the present day, consists in introducing the colours required, without any reference to their being found in nature or not.

CUYP'S PRINCIPLE

CHAPTER II.

SECTION I.

CUYP'S PRINCIPLE.

The simplest arrangement and treatment of Colours will be found in the style of Cuyp and Both; objects in shadow are relieved against a warm sunny sky. For the reasons given in the Sketcher's Manual, with regard to Progressive Execution, these are the best adapted to beginners; objects in shadow do not present much variety of tint.

The whole aspect or general tone of the picture is warm. The shadows are cooler than the lights, but very far from cold; being of a Sepia brown, and sometimes warmer, with some cool reflections from the air. The sky is gently graduated from a rich yellow to the most delicate warm grey. The middle ground affords some blackish-green half-tints or shadows; and some golden lights are introduced in front.

Cuyp treated figures, animals, and boats in this way. The points requiring attention and care are, first, the tone of the sky and yellow lights, which must be obtained from yellow and Roman ochres; the sky should have a creamy quality of colour; and what little grey is introduced, must be Cobalt Blue, or Ultramarine with Carmine, or Lake, so as to prevent the slightest appearance of green; secondly, the masses of shadow must be of agreeable shape and must not be too dark. Plate.

BOTH'S PRINCIPLE

CHAPTER II.

SECTION II.

BOTH'S PRINCIPLE.

The style of Both is only a slight variation from that of Cuyp. He adopted a different character of subject, usually contriving to relieve a mass of rock or bank, and a tree with delicate foliage against the sky; and he increased the warmth of the general aspect of the picture, by making the tree and part of another *light* bank, of the rich brown afforded by burnt Terra de Sienna, and by introducing some red clouds in the sky. In some instances Both has not escaped the dangers that present the difficulty to his followers; the tone of these pictures appears hot, and thereby a vulgarity is occasioned, and that refinement which is required by Taste in the Fine Arts, is destroyed. Plate.

RUYSDAEL'S AND HOBBIMA'S PRINCIPLE

CHAPTER II.
SECTION III.
HOBBIMA AND RUYSDAEL'S PRINCIPLES.

These masters have adopted a style which, though apparently as opposite to that of Cuyp and Both as cold is to warm, resembles it in this respect—they rarely, if ever, admit positive colours in force, and thus offer another simple principle for the treatment and arrangement of tints.

In Hobbima and Ruysdael, who painted landscapes, dark brownish masses are relieved against a cloudy grey sky, and some white or grey light is introduced in front to carry the colour of the sky through the work. The general aspect of the picture is cold. What little warmth of tone may be admitted, is to be found in the centre of the shadows; and the only approximation to positive colour, is in the sky, a little cold feeble blue, obtained in water-colours from Indigo; and a small portion of a deeper shade of the same tone of blue on mountains or trees in shadow in the distance; or a little cold green in the middle ground. If ever any red be introduced, it must be a mere speck of vermilion shaded with grey, to give value by contrast to the neutral tones, which make up the principle part of the picture. Plate.

OSTADE'S PRINCIPLE

CHAPTER II.

SECTION IV.

TENIERS AND OSTADE'S PRINCIPLES.

Teniers and Ostade have treated homely interiors upon the same principle, making up the greater part of the picture with brownish grey tones, and introducing in the light, some very feeble spots of the primary colours, carefully shaded with grey, to assimilate them with the general aspect of the work. What little warmth is admitted, is found in the shadows and reflections, as in the productions of Ruysdael and Hobbima. But the lights afford a greater purity of tone; so that while the works of Ruysdael and Hobbima would be said to have a grey tone, Teniers, and particularly Ostade, are said to have a silvery tone. Plate.

PRINCIPLE OF TITIAN AND THE VENETIAN SCHOOL

CHAPTER II.

SECTION V.

THE PRINCIPLES OF TITIAN AND THE VENETIAN SCHOOL.

The Venetian School, founded by Titian, adopted a combination of rich warm browns, yellows, and greens, supported by crimsons, all deep in tone, overspreading two-thirds of the picture, opposed by very rich, almost warm, blues, and animated by a point of white, sometimes accompanied by black in the front of the subject. No violent contrasts are admitted, no crude colours. The white is toned down to assimilate with flesh tints, which are again toned to accord with golden lights, gradually deepening into yellowish browns, and emerging through warm greens to join the blues, which are kept in check by the opposition in some places to rich reddish browns of the same relative shade, so that one shall not be darker than the other; the blue is graduated as it approaches the white, into which it is blended by the interposition of fleshy-coloured tints. The whole aspect of the picture is rich and warm, but subdued. The lights are golden and the shadows brown, with just so much cool green,

18

white, and blue, as shall prevent the picture appearing rusty. But though these tints are called cool, because they are cooler than the rest of the work, as in the style of Cuyp and Both, they must not be cold; but above all it is requisite to take care that they are not crude. White must be toned with yellow or red; blue must incline to purple; and if black be introduced, it must not be *blue* black. Plate.

LUDOVICO CARACCI'S PRINCIPLE

CHAPTER II.

SECTION VI.

LUDOVICO CARACCI'S PRINCIPLE.

Ludovico Caracci followed the Venetian school, but subdued the colours of the whole picture, to what Sir Joshua Reynolds calls a "cloistered tone," the effect of a "dim religious light, through storied pane." Neither white nor black are admitted: the deepest shadows do not descend below a rich brown; the brightest lights do not rise above a creamy yellow. The blue is no longer opposed to a brown of the same relative shade, but is introduced in the half-lights, and carefully blended into the shadows, by means of warm reflections, and the interposition of reddish purple shadows. The Chiaroscuro is broader and more tranquil than in the works of the Venetian school. Plate.

ANOTHER PRINCIPLE OF TITIAN

CHAPTER II.
SECTION VII.
ANOTHER PRINCIPLE OF TITIAN.

Titian has adopted another principle in the painted ceiling of the Hall of Judgment, in the Ducal palace at Venice. Pure greys are interspersed amongst masses of bright crimson, which are opposed to some pure white and blue, broken by flesh tints. The reds and greys are supported by some warm yellows, and the whole assimilated by rich brown shadows. The contrasts of colour and Chiaroscuro are vivid, and require care in the shapes, as well as the situations of the masses and points of relief. Plate.

This principle of colouring is applicable to gorgeous historical subjects, portraits, and flowers. Sir Thomas Lawrence frequently adopted it with a slight variation, resulting from the combination of some portion of the following principle which was developed by Rubens.

CHAPTER II.

SECTION VIII.

RUBENS' PRINCIPLE.

Rubens is the founder of another school in which the most violent contrasts of colour and Chiaroscuro are admitted in the focus of the picture. The deepest black, supported by rich yellows, crimsons, and blues, is opposed to the brightest vermilion, sometimes heightened with gold, and the purest white, which is graduated through every variety of pearly tint into bright blues, interspersed with purply greys, creamy and fleshy half-tints.

Great simplicity of Chiaroscuro is requisite in this style of colouring. Both the white and the black must graduate uninterruptedly into the half-lights, which form the greater part of the picture. The crimsons, blues, and yellows, that support the black, must all partake of the same tone. The vermilion must graduate into purply tints, which will emerge through greys and greens to the bright blue. Plate.

TURNER'S PRINCIPLE

CHAPTER II.
SECTION IX.
TURNER'S PRINCIPLE.

Turner has controverted the old doctrine of a balance of colours, by showing that a picture may be made up of delicately graduated blues and white, supported by pale cool green, and enlivened by a point of rich brownish crimson. It requires some care in the graduation and shapes of the masses of blue and white, and in the situation of the point of colour. Plate.

ANOTHER PRINCIPLE OF TURNER

CHAPTER II.

SECTION X.

ANOTHER PRINCIPLE OF TURNER.

Another principle adopted by Turner is, to contrast rich autumnal yellows in the foreground, with a brilliant Italian blue sky, graduated through a series of exquisitely delicate pearly tints, to meet the cooler green tints of the middle ground. The warm colours in the foreground are qualified by purply half-tints, and supported by warm shadows and some rich crimsons; or sometimes reduced to comparative sobriety by the opposition of the brightest orange and white. Plate.

MODERN MANNER

CHAPTER II.

SECTION XI.

MODERN MANNER.

A very favourite manner of the present day is partially to relieve a tower, steeple, spire, or some upright object, rendered of a purple colour, against a white cloud which is graduated with purply greys, creamy and fleshy tints, and opposed to some bright patches of blue; the lower part of the building or object is graduated through cool greens or greys, into some warmer yellows or browns in the foreground, which are interspersed with points of bright colours, such as Cobalt blue, Vermilion, Lake, and sometimes white and black, but always introducing in front some dull red, as of bricks or tiles, contrasted with fresh greys. Plate.

CHAPTER II.

SECTION XII.

ABSTRACT PRINCIPLES TO WHICH THESE

ARRANGEMENTS MAY BE REFERRED.

These several styles of colouring may be reduced to certain abstract principles, which may be made the foundation for other and different arrangements, as the taste and talent of the artist or amateur may dictate.

Pictures may be made up of a balance, or harmonic arrangement of TONES.

Or, of a balance, or harmonic arrangement of COLOURS.

Or, of a balance, or harmonic arrangement of TONES and COLOURS.

Or, by relieving a SPARK of COLOUR against a mass of TONES.

Or, by relieving a spot of black or white, *the concentration of* TONES, against a general aspect of COLOURS.

Pictures may be warm in tone, qualified by so much cool tint as will prevent their appearing hot.

Or cool, with so much warm tint as will prevent their appearing cold.

A small spark of bright colour will balance a large mass of subdued tint. Equal brightness will require equal masses.

For the principles by which the shapes and situations of masses and points must be governed, the reader is referred to the Sketcher's Manual, where they will be found at length, and carefully illustrated. The same regulations that govern the distribution of several lights or shadows, must guide the positions of several masses of the same colour. If two or more are introduced, they must not be equal in size, nor similar in shape, nor must they be so placed, that a line drawn through them, would be either horizontal or vertical—parallel with either base or side. The great principle of colouring being Variety within the limits of Harmony, such masses of similar tints should be of different sizes and shapes, and should be interspersed at different distances through the picture, so as to suggest an undulating line, traversing all, or at least three, of the four quarters of the picture, that all the particular colour shall not be on one side, and none on the other, nor all at the lower, and none in the upper half of the picture. But if the arrangement of relieving a spark of colour against a mass of tones, or the reverse be adopted, it must not be placed in the centre of the picture, nor equidistant from either top and base, or the two sides.

With regard to the beauty of individual tints, it would be difficult to come to any very strict definition, as what is pleasing to one person, is not so to another; and particularly in reference to the use of colours in Art, for they then become so dependent upon the other tints by which they are surrounded, that they may be said to cease to have positive designations, and to become only comparative; and there is scarcely any tint, however disagreeable in itself, but may be made by Art to appear agreeable, if not beautiful. But the object of the present work being to collect the certain or decided principles of Art, for the benefit of those who desire to derive pleasure or amusement from it, the doubtful or questionable hypotheses will be left untouched, and those points only brought forward which are calculated to ensure success.

For this purpose, the amateur should avoid greenish blues and greenish yellows; they both appear sickly: and never place such a green between blue and yellow as would result from the mixture of the particular tints of those two colours which are made use of.

Both blue and yellow become agreeable as they incline to red. Red becomes rich as it inclines to blue, brilliant as it inclines to yellow. All shades and tones of purple or orange are agreeable; but of greens, those only which incline to yellow. Blueish greens require either to be very pale, as shown in Turner's first principle (*See Plate*), or moderated with black, so as almost to cease to be colours, and become tones. All shades and tints of the tertiary compounds are agreeable in their places; they receive value by the opposition of the colour which enters least into their composition, and become difficult to manage only when they approach full blueish green.

White and black give value to all colours and tones.

It may be necessary to make an observation upon the foregoing warning, and almost proscription, of the use of green in Art, as that colour is found to be exceedingly agreeable in Nature, and is used with success in manufactures, and for other general purposes. It is found to afford great relief to weak sight, and is abstractedly so much admired, that it appears singular and paradoxical to say, that green must be sparingly used in pictures, even in landscapes, whose greatest charm in nature consist of luxuriance of vegetation: but such is the case. The general tone of a picture may be yellow, as in the works of Cuyp, Both, Ludovico Caracci (*see Plates*); red, as in the second principle of Titian (*see Plate*); blue, as in the first principle of Turner (*see Plates*); grey or brown, as in the works of Ruysdael and the Dutch School (*see Plates*); but a green picture, however true to nature, instantly excites an universal outcry as being disagreeable; and if any of the modern school, to which we shall presently advert, have been for a moment tolerated, it has arisen from the previous great reputation of the artist, or for other merits in the work, and in *spite* of its being a green picture.

The following hypothesis *may* be the mode of accounting for this paradox, and, at the same time, *may* throw some light upon another, which will be noticed; that although painting is an imitative art, imitation, to the extent of deception, does not constitute its highest excellence.

The eye is excited by Colour, and the object of painting, independent of poetical expression or character, is to excite the eye agreeably. But green is found to excite the eye *less* than any other tint, (thereby affording some corroboration to the idea that, strictly speaking, its opposite red, is the only true *colour*,) not even excepting black; so that it acts as an opiate, and is used for counteracting the brightness of the sun, by means of parasols or glasses, and to guard weak eyes from the effects of light by means of silk shades.

It is thrown out as a suggestion that, in looking at a picture in which excitement to the degree of pleasure is *expected*, a disappointment *may* arise from finding a prevalence of those tints which do not excite, except to a very slight extent, and that *thus* a green picture *may* occasion dissatisfaction. In looking at Nature we do not wish to be always excited, and green is admired or valued as affording repose; but in looking at a picture, the very object is excitement, within certain limits, which green has a tendency to destroy.

Certain tints of green become disagreeable in certain parts of pictures, from association of ideas. Green in flesh, excites the idea of corruption and decay. Green in skies, occasioned by blending the warm yellows of sunset with the blue, excite the impression of want of skill to prevent the one tint running into the other.

But in reservation it must be repeated, that there is no tint that cannot be controlled and made available, by great skill and management, to the purposes of Art. These warnings are for beginners and amateurs; and the work is intended to show them what they may do with safety; as they attain proficiency, they may attempt difficulties, which principally reside in *truth* of detail *in combination* with agreeable general effect. When to this is added a just subservience to Poetical Character, the greatest requisitions of the Art have been complied with; all other difficulties, of whatever nature, being merely a species of mountebank trickery, beneath the aim of high Art, and deserving of the well-known sarcasm of Dr. Johnson upon some difficult music, that "he wished it were impossible."

CHAPTER III.

FINE COLOURING.

Having shown in the preceding chapters certain principles upon which Pictorial arrangements of Colours may be ensured, the attention of the reader must be directed to what other qualities are requisite to constitute Fine Colouring.

Fine Colouring must not be confounded with Fine Colours. Some of the Finest Colourists have avoided Fine Colours, and Sir Joshua Reynolds adduces as a *proof* that Apelles was a Fine Colourist, the statement by Pliny, that, "after he had finished his pictures, he passed an *atramentum*, or blackness, over the whole of them."

Nor is truth of imitation sufficient of itself to constitute Fine Colouring, though it always confers a value on a work of Art.

Fine Colouring, in the higher walks of Art, implies an adaptation of the general aspect or style of colouring to the expression and character of the subject; it then acquires the title of Poetical Colouring, which is its highest commendation as a means of Art.

But, independent of subject, there are other abstract qualifications of Fine Colouring to be sought for, in the representation of objects. It not only requires such an arrangement of tints and tones as shall produce an agreeable whole, but descends to minutiæ, and demands that such tints and tones, shall be obtained by a degree of refinement or idealization, within probability, of the ordinary appearances of Nature, or by a selection of the greatest beauties she displays, and such a combination of them as shall contribute to convey the most pleasing impressions, and present *her* under the most attractive aspect.

CHAPTER III.

SECTION I.

PRINCIPLES OF COLOURING OBJECTS.

Proceeding to consider Colouring independently of Character or Expression, to which it should be subservient in the higher walks of Art, the attention of the reader must be directed to a circumstance connected with truth of representation.

It has commonly been the practice, under the almost universal sanction of great authorities, to place the student who may be desirous of acquiring the Art of Painting, before some object, and to direct him to copy *what he sees*. But what does he see?

We need not go into the question of *how* impressions are produced upon the mind, through the medium of the eye; whether a species of picture of the object be, during the inspection, as it were painted upon the retina; and whether that be inverted or anywise different from the real object; or whether, and to what extent, association rectifies the imperfections of our sight. These, and other investigations into the philosophical and physical nature of vision, may be left to the consideration of those who desire to account for particular facts; we have to do with the facts themselves.

In whatever manner the effect may be produced, it is indisputable, that a certain and distinct impression is produced upon the mind, through the medium of the eye, by every object which may be before it, and that impression has a strict relation to the real character of the object; for instance, a marble statue, it appears, or an impression is conveyed of, an object of one unvaried tint. How this impression is conveyed, is of no consequence; it is conveyed; and a series of tints may be artificially arranged upon paper (or any other convenient material), so as also, if not equally, to convey to the mind the impression of a marble statue of uniform whiteness. But upon examination of the drawing or painting, it would be seen, that scarcely any two parts of the *representation* of the statue were of exactly the same tint. Some parts would be delicately graduated from a point of light, through a series of darker tints, to give the appearance of roundness; while others would be made nearly black by shadow, to give the appearance of projection. The present enquiry has reference solely to Colours, but the same difficulties occur with regard to forms.

Here there is a discrepancy, occasioned by Association, which we shall scarcely find language to explain, but which will in most cases prove of serious perplexity to the student; for there are some other persons like Queen Elizabeth, who have no idea of shadow, unless it be the shadow of a parasol or tree, under which they may escape the intensity of a noon-day sun. The statue will appear, or an impression will be conveyed to the mind, of uniform whiteness. But pictorially speaking, one spot only, that which reflects the greatest light, will appear quite white. All the other parts will *appear*, that is, to convey the impression, they must be made, of an infinite variety of tints, from the brightest light to the deepest shadow. The statue *is* actually uniformly white, and it appears uniformly white, yet the *appearance* or representation which must be put upon paper, to convey an impression of that *appearance* by drawing or painting, is totally opposite, being an infinite variety of tints.

But in a statue, by reason of its convexity, the second species of *appearance*, the Pictorial, is much more readily appreciated, from the strong opposition of light and shadow, than in a flat surface,—a ceiling, a pavement, or meadow, in which the perception of the modifications of colour, arising from what is termed aerial perspective, is considerably influenced, by the Association above mentioned, until the eye has become educated to observe these minute and delicate gradations of tint. Thus, in looking at a meadow, we know the grass to be generally of the same colour throughout, and to an uneducated eye it *appears* equally green from one end to the other: or the ceiling of a well lighted room, we know it to be of one colour throughout, and it *appears* of one even tint from the nearest to the most distant extremity; yet pictorially speaking, it *appears* of an infinite variety of tints, for the effect of the atmosphere is such as to rob the grass of its colour, and to make the white ceiling grey, as they recede from the eye.

It will scarcely be necessary to guard against misconception as to the use of the terms describing the effect of the atmosphere, by explaining that it is not intended to assert that an *actual change* takes place, or that there is any *actual* difference in the colour of those parts of objects which are at a distance from the eye; or, that the colour in the distance does not appear to be, as we know it is, the same with that nearest the eye; but that the effect of distance is the *pictorial appearance* of a modification of tint, by the interposition of the atmosphere, perceptible only to an educated eye.

We know the grass to be equally green throughout, and it appears of the tints which convey that impression; while Association conceals the modification occasioned by the interposition of the atmosphere (which the generality of observers consider as only "air," and of no consequence), and excites the notion that the meadow appears of one equal flat tint. But the distant extremity of the meadow is seen through more or less atmosphere, which is more or less dense; and in proportion to its density will the colour of the grass be *apparently* altered or changed thereby; and in some instances, as in case of a fog, entirely concealed.

In looking at any object through a perfectly transparent medium, such as plate glass, we do not perceive any alteration in the real colours. But when the medium is not perfectly transparent, which is the case with the atmosphere, the colours of all objects seen through it are modified or tinged in proportion to its density, until they are sometimes lost or absorbed in the tint of the medium.

The slightest possible colourless opacity gives a medium approaching to a whitish film, which is very evident when there is light behind it; as in the case of the beams of the moon. This is the clearest state of the atmosphere. As it increases in density, it becomes more and more white, until it becomes a white mist, fog or cloud. The atmosphere is sometimes coloured, as will hereafter be mentioned; at present we have to do with its colourless state.

The opacity of the atmosphere, as a white film over the darkness of space, occasions the blue appearance of the sky; and in proportion to the rarity or density of the medium, is the intensity of colour, or rather depth of tone. If the atmosphere be extremely rare, as in the Polar regions, or at the height of Mont Blanc, the sky appears almost black. And if the atmosphere be thick with vapour, the sky assumes a milky colour, and the blue tint is lost in that of the medium. When the atmosphere is just so rare as to be scarcely perceptible in its influence upon terrestrial objects,—as in Italy, or the eastern climes, where the most distant buildings appear diminished in size, but almost as distinct as those close to the spectator,—yet sufficiently dense to become a veil to the expanse of space, the colour of the sky appears the most intense blue. As near as we can superficially ascertain it,—in the exact medium between such rarity of atmosphere as would afford blackness, and such opacity as would afford whiteness,—we may expect to find the most intensely blue colour in the sky.

As the effect of this colourless opacity of the atmosphere is, to render the appearance of the *darkness of space* a blue colour, so all dark terrestrial objects are similarly affected by the intervening of this medium, and, in a corresponding degree, become more or less blue. The dark mountains in Wales and Scotland appear of a deep blue, sometimes verging upon purple; and a slight comparison between the colour of the trees close to the spectator and those in the distance, will show how much more blue the latter become, from the influence of the medium through which they are viewed.

And as objects, in proportion to their distance, are more or less affected by the interposition of the atmosphere, so, also, do the parts of the individual objects themselves, become more or less grey as they recede. The boundaries of a white object are less white, and of a black object less black, than the parts nearest the eye. A tree is most green at the prominent parts, and greyer at the top and sides.

This truth is so decidedly felt by the public in general—though perhaps insensibly appreciated and but tacitly acknowledged,—that, as the atmosphere reduces the colours of all objects to a blue tint, so all blue colours convey an impression of distance, and all tints approaching to blue are accordingly designated *retiring colours*.

But the atmosphere is not always colourless. The rays of the sun tinge it with yellow. The rays from a fire or candle tinge it with a colour approaching to red. The combination of smoke tinges it with black or brown; and fogs infuse various degrees of dingy yellow. All these variations affect the colours of the objects seen through the atmosphere, and modify the degree of blue, or quality of grey, tint communicated thereby.

When the atmosphere is coloured by the light of the sun, the blue is modified, more or less, into a warm grey. But owing to the brilliancy resulting from the blaze of light, the tints remain of the utmost purity. All tendency to green is kept in subordination by the pearly tints of those parts which are in shadow. The atmosphere is rendered more dense at the same time that it is coloured by the light of the sun; but the light parts of the objects seen through it are rendered, by the same cause, so much more brilliant, that the density of the medium is partially compensated; while its full effect is apparent upon the shadows seen through it, over which a bright haze diffuses a beautiful blue tint, slightly warmed by the golden colour of the illuminating power. The contrast of the yellow tinge in the lights makes these shadows appear to incline to purple; and at sunset and sunrise, when by the greater quantity of the medium, rendered more dense by the aqueous vapours close to the earth, the colour of the sun's light is enriched to a deep golden hue approaching orange and red, the shadows assume a decidedly purple tint, of which the blue is supplied by the density, and the red by the colour, of the medium. As the light of the sun decreases, the colour of the atmosphere is more evidently tinged with red, until the sun has sunk so far below the horizon, that the shadows of night incorporating with the colour of the vapours, render them a dull grey, sometimes approaching a brown.

In proportion as the atmosphere is illumined does it also become opaque. The sky close to the sun appears much less blue than on the opposite side of the heavens. The beams of the sun, or moon, or even the rays of a candle, become so opaque, as absolutely to conceal all objects behind them.

In a glowing sunshine, the particles of the atmosphere loaded with light, produce that soft haze or *caligine*, "as the Italian hath it," by which the colours of every object seen through it, are assimilated in one broad, warm, grey tone, however varied the tints of the objects in reality may be.

Another singular appearance takes place in remote objects, of which no one has so fully availed himself as Turner, for the production of pictorial beauties, and the brilliancy of sunshine. The atmosphere, which becomes most visible when before shadows, is frequently so much illuminated by the sun's rays, as to make the shadows appear nearly equally light with the illuminated parts of the objects; and the only distinction between the lights and shadows is to be found in the difference of tint—the shadows being blue or purple, and the lights a warm yellow, or fleshy colour.

The practice in art, both in Oil and in Water colours, has been an imitation of the process of nature, and with similar results. It is usual in Oil to paint the distance stronger in colour than it is intended to remain, and when dry, to pass some very thin opaque colour (technically to scumble) over the whole. Thus the most perfectly aerial tints are produced. In Water Colours, owing to the different quality of the materials employed, another method is adopted. White, or any opaque pigment (except when used in conjunction with Oil painting), has a disagreeable effect; so it is considered advisable partially to wash out the too highly coloured distance, and aerial tints similar to those produced by the scumble are obtained.

However requisite it may be philosophically to account for these appearances, it is unnecessary to perplex the reader of the present work with a questionable statement of the greater impetus of rays of certain colours enabling them to penetrate through the dense atmosphere, while others are more feeble, and are swallowed up and absorbed by the medium through which they in vain essay to pass. This may be a very pretty story to amuse children with, and such philosophers as are verging on their second childhood; but while so simple a method can be discovered of accounting for the blueness of the sky and distant objects, and one that can be so easily exemplified as that given in the previous pages, we shall not be the parties to contribute to that amusement, by writing "the history of some blue rays that were lost in a fog." Nor is this the place to point out the absurdity of such theories; it will be sufficient to remark that *if* they are correct, all distant objects must appear *red*; and the blueness of the sky can only be accounted for by the hypothesis, that the atmosphere is a sort of trap for the blue rays of all the light that has passed and is passing through it!

Such being the effect of the atmosphere, and such being the antagonizing influence of Association in looking at Nature, it has been found necessary for the purposes of Art, in representation, to exaggerate the former, to overstep the modesty of Nature, and thus to produce what may be termed conventional imitations or translations of Nature.

For, in looking at a picture, Association again affects us; and as we know what is before us to be a flat surface, this can only be overcome by increasing the effects produced by atmospheric influence, reflections, refractions, &c. Hence the colour of all distant objects are reduced to some tone of grey, oscillating between the extremes of bright blue or even purple, and the medium between black and white as the subject, may be in sunshine cold daylight; or, as the taste of the artist may lead him to prefer one scale of colouring to another. Those who delight in the sunny skies of Italy, or tropical climates, represent the distance by the purest blue that Ultramarine affords. Others, who delineate the village church or cathedral tower, represent them of a dark grey. Mountain scenery is represented of a deep Indigo blue, sometimes inclining to a decided purple, as all must remember in the drawings of the late Mr. Robson.

If this exaggeration or pictorial license be objected to, as an unnecessary departure from truth or the beauty of Nature, let the most inveterate worshipper of verisimilitude place himself before a landscape under bright sunshine, on a clear day, and make an exact representation, if he be able, of what he sees; and he will be convinced that in such an instance, something more and very different is required, to make a finely coloured picture. It cannot be that the colours of the original are deficient in beauty, but that an essential quality of the beauty of Nature cannot be preserved by Imitative Art. He will find that it will not be possible to preserve even slightly the gradation of tints before him, without descending almost to blackness in the shadows, which will be destructive of brilliancy of sunshine, and at the same time, of that quality which is indispensable in a work of Art, *breadth*. He will find that in comparison with the brightness of the sky, the trees will look as dark as they are represented by Ruysdael and Hobbima, but who incontestibly do not give the idea of sunshine. As in translating from one language to another, he will find that a literal version may give the bones, but not the spirit of the text; and that something more is required to transfer the full force and character of the original. Herein consists a great part of the art of colouring objects. It may be that the scene being unbounded in Nature, is acted upon by extraneous circumstances which cannot be called to the aid of a picture.

As it is impossible with pigments to rival the brightness of light, it has been found necessary to adopt some method of forcing the effect of colours, so as to conceal or to supply a compensation for this deficiency, and *apparently* to produce the vigour of truth.

This has led to a division, which rivals in fierceness as in name, the feud of the Bianchi and the Neri of Italy, into two great schisms or factions of colourists, of whom, it is to be regretted, too many are apt to consider those of the opposite party as lost in the depths of absurdity. The hostility and contempt are quite mutual, and equally ungrounded.

A writer in Blackwood's Magazine of the Neri faction says, "We have received a prescriptive right to make war upon the rising heresy of light pictures, and we will wage it to the knife," or some such expressions.

Certain tones of colour have been found to be almost universally recognized as agreeables; and by the above mentioned class of artists and critics, the Neri, it is held to be "fine colouring," to reduce every representation, without consideration of propriety, to these conventionally agreeable tones. Plate. Sir Joshua Reynolds commends a picture of a moonlight scene by Rubens, which is so rich in colour, that if you hide the moon it appears like a sunset.

The background of the far-famed Mercury, Venus and Cupid, by Corregio, in the National Gallery, and the sky of the Bacchus and Ariadne, by Titian, in the same collection, are instances of this practice, the use of conventionally agreeable tones, which may be seen by every one. It would be difficult to say what the former was meant for, except *background* to the figures; and no one ever saw a sky such a blue as the latter. It irresistibly brings to mind the counter-criticism of a sceptic to the admiration of a landscape by Poussin, in which Sir ——, a worshipper of the old masters, was indulging:—"What I like so much is, it looks so *like* an *old picture*."—"Yes," said the sceptic, "and the *sky* looks as *old* as the *rest* of the *picture*, for you never see such a sky now-a-days."

The Neri apparently give up all hope of rivalling the brightness of nature; but by forcing the shadows and general tone of the whole picture, endeavour to produce the same *gradation* of light and shadow as in nature, but on a lower scale.

The Bianchi party, on the other hand, endeavour to compensate for the want of positive brilliancy, by refining or increasing the delicacy and beauty of the tints.

Light is the origin, or immediate cause of *colour*, and the brighter the light, the greater variety of tints will be found or displayed. As we cannot rival the cause, the Bianchi contend that we must increase the effect by introducing *colour* in lieu of those *tints* which in nature appear neutral; and thus conceal the weakness of our imitation of the cause, by making it apparently produce greater effects. Thus all greys are rendered by pure Ultramarine blue tints, or delicate pearly purple, and the greatest possible variety of beautiful and delicate colours are introduced in the light; while the shadows are generally of a neutral colour, the most decidedly contrasting with the tints in the light. But sometimes the colour is also carried through the shadows as well as the lights; positive crimson being introduced into those of leaves or grass; while those of flesh are rendered by a dull red; and those of a sandy bank by pure blue. Plate.

The Neri complain that the Bianchi want tone, and the Bianchi that the Neri want purity and light.

Each of these factions contends, that all the difficulty of fine colouring is to be found only in their own aim; while they hold in perfect contempt the productions of their opponents, as being of such facile achievement as to the sarcasm of Michael Angelo,—to be "fit only for children," and beneath the attention of those who profess to study the Fine Arts.

THE NERI

The main difference between the principles of these two parties or factions, will be found to lie in the treatment of the atmospheric influence and association, previously alluded to. The Bianchi availing themselves of the former circumstance, as a reason for introducing a great variety of pearly greys, on the purity and beauty of which they contend fine colouring is dependent; and the Neri availing themselves of the latter, as an excuse for the introduction of breadth of warm tones, and the omission of as much as possible of the cool tints, which are deemed so indispensable by their rivals; they limit the representation of atmospheric influence to the least possible degree. Titian's Venuses are masses of the local colour of flesh, broken with so little half-tint, that they are scarcely round, and satisfy few but critics sufficiently learned in the Art, to be contented with the beauties of *Art*, as a substitute for the imitation of *Nature*.

This class of colouring is founded upon the power of Association, previously alluded to, by which, the local colour overpowers the greys of atmospheric influence; in other words, that to the eyes of the many, *flesh* looks of a *flesh* colour, and ought to be so represented. But the *full* effect of Association is here not allowed for. In looking at flesh, we know it to be flesh colour; and we know it to be round; and it requires some education of the eye to discover the atmospheric influence, as well as the minute gradations in form. But on the other hand, in looking at a picture, we know it to be a flat surface; and however far the *imagination* may be willing or have a tendency to supply the deficiencies in the representation, *Association* is an *antagonist* and not an ally. This will become evident upon making outlines of objects and filling them up with flat tints; imagination will not have power to make them appear to be round, or to recede. The beauties of this class of colouring are solely conventional.

Titian, Giorgione, and Sir Joshua Reynolds lead the van of the Neri; Rubens, Vandyke, and Lawrence are at the head of the Bianchi; unless, indeed, we should consider Turner as general-in-chief of the latter. Claude was probably of the Bianchi faction; but Time, who is the great ally of the Neri, has made him appear in some of his productions an adherent of that party.

It may be added, that most historical painters lean to the Neri faction, on account of the disadvantage arising from too close an approach to the common appearance of every-day nature, of which the effect is described in the proverb, that "familiarity breeds contempt," and consequently is destructive of that grandeur, solemnity, or refinement which is indispensable in high art; and they take refuge in the "cloistered tone" of Ludovico Caracci, so commended by Sir Joshua Reynolds, a conventional beauty which will presently be noticed. The Landscape painters, on the other hand, almost universally belong to the Bianchi party; as truth or *apparent* truth is so much more indispensable in subjects that only display the scenery of nature, and which depend upon that resemblance for producing an impression, than in subjects which appeal to the passions by the display of some stirring incident. From the nature of the materials employed, the tendency of oil painting is to the side of the Neri; whilst the general inclination induced by Water-colour drawing, is in favour of the Bianchi party. The *alleged* principle of the colouring of the Neri is deduced from the hypothesis laid down by Sir Isaac Newton, that neither white nor black are *colours*, therefore say the Neri, "neither should appear in a finely coloured picture; the brightest lights should not be white; the deepest shadows should not be black;" nevertheless, those productions which are cited by this party as the finest specimens of colour in existence, *do* contain both *white* and *black*. In the celebrated picture by Giorgione, copied recently by Mr. Ward, R.A., to the eye of the uninitiated are presented both white lights, and black shadows. The former, it is true, are reduced by *Time* or glazing; and the latter are excused as having lost their original colour.

But this principle can scarcely be said to be carried out, except in such pictures as possess the "cloistered tone" of Ludovico Caracci alluded to. Here the lights are warm and golden, as if transmitted through stained glass. The atmospheric greys are introduced to no greater extent than is indispensable to prevent the picture appearing rusty. The shadows are deep rich browns, into which are thrown still warmer reflections; and the whole picture is subdued to a soft-mysterious effect, which is admirably adapted to produce what is technically termed *repose*, and to excite gentle, reverential, solemn, and even affectionate feelings. It is a style of colouring peculiarly suited to religious subjects; and in representations of interiors, may be said to be like nature, because Nature *may* be made to appear like it. (*See Plate.*)

THE BIANCHI

This principle of colouring may be carried out on a higher scale than is generally found among the productions of its advocates, and abstractedly, is undoubtedly calculated to lead to very beautiful results; though it may be questioned, whether it is sufficient to entitle the party exclusively to arrogate to themselves the designation of *colourists*, as they are in the habit of doing. For the principle of the Bianchi is likewise adapted to produce exceedingly beautiful colouring; and without some rational or scientific standard by which the comparative beauty of individual colours may be determined, so as to distinguish between fine colours and fine colouring, the admirers of this class of colours may, with the greatest justice, contend that it is equally beautiful with that of the opposite party; while it has this superiority, that it will enable the Artist to produce much more resemblance in the representation of *external* nature, and will be much less artificial in the effects produced as imitation of interiors.

And they derive a strong argument in favour of their mode of proceeding being correct, and most likely to stand, from the circumstance, that the pictures of Vandyke, many of which are *now* claimed by the Neri as painted on their principle, when first done were frequently censured as being too *raw* or *white*.

Further, it should be observed that, by too many of the Neri party, their great object of worship, *Tone*, is limited to the rich warm brownish yellow which is legitimately superinduced in oil pictures by the action of Time, or glazing; and surreptitiously obtained by washing with tobacco-water. But an inspection of the works of the Dutch school, who belong to a third party which considers both the Bianchi and Neri to be in the wrong, as too artificial, will show that *tone* may be cool as well as warm, and that there is a silvery *tone* which has as devoted admirers as those of the Golden Image—(*see Plates of Ruysdael and of Ostade*).

THE DUTCH SCHOOL

It may not be becoming in the author of the present work to decide between these great disputants; but from the statement respecting Vandyke's pictures, that they were considered *raw* when fresh painted, as well as from the nature of the materials employed, it is evident, that the productions of Titian, Giorgione, and other celebrated colourists, were not, when first painted, of such deep tones as they exhibit now; and it may be suspected that the reputation, which was derived from the *original* colouring of their pictures, has, to a certain extent, been attached to the colouring they at present exhibit; and that veneration of talent, and respect for authority, have given sanction to what would be repudiated by the Great men whose names form the slogan of the party, and is not really entitled to commendation.

That the two principles may be combined, and so produce higher qualities than either affords alone, is hardly possible, when their opposite treatment of the effects of atmospheric influence and association are taken into consideration.

But this compromise may be made between them with advantage both to Amateurs and Artists; that the style of the Neri, including that of the Dutch school, may be considered as most applicable to the representation of interiors and quiet or grand subjects; while that of the Bianchi may be considered as most suited to exteriors, and subjects of gaiety and animation.

For the benefit of the Amateur, it will be necessary to say something more upon the style of colouring adopted by the Dutch school, the productions of which among the cognoscenti, are termed pictures of *Tone*; tone being in this instance used in opposition to positive colour, and as implying varieties of the ternary combinations, called neutral tints, or greys, but otherwise possessing the qualities of tone in a general sense, namely, transparency.

This style of colouring is peculiarly adapted to the class of subjects on which the Masters of the Dutch school generally exercised their pencils, homely interiors; but when applied to out-of-door scenes, although undoubtedly possessed of certain conventional beauties, such as harmonious arrangement and balance of tones, it has a tendency to look dull and heavy. The landscapes of Ruysdael and Hobbima do not reckon among their beauties, that of vivacity or cheerfulness. They may be clear and bright and fresh, as their admirers say, but they do not represent Nature under her most bewitching aspect, nor is the style of the school adapted to do so. It leans to the side of the Neri, from its dread of brilliant colours. It is unaffected, sober, and in many instances, such as interiors or close woody scenes under grey daylight, possesses great truth; but from its limited application, and unpretending effect, is scarcely to be put into competition, as a style of Fine Colouring, with the higher aims of the two great parties before mentioned. Plate.

Such is the present state of the theory of Fine Colouring; from which it is evident, that, except in a very limited class of subjects, Truth *cannot* be made the test—that even in this class of subjects, it is disputed whether it *should* be made the test; and that it is also disputed, to what extent a departure from truth is admissible; or rather, what quantity of resemblance to Nature is indispensable, and what method may be the best of compensating the want of accurate transcription; in short, what is the true *idiom* of Fine Colouring in Art, so as fully to translate the beauties of Nature.

The fashion of the day rather leans to the Bianchi party in Water-colour drawings, if not in Oil paintings; but the principles of *none* of the parties are *fully* developed in the works of their existing followers. The followers of the Dutch school are sacrificing part of their truth for some, but it may be doubted whether the best, part of the conventional tones of both the other parties. The Bianchi are more regardless of truth than they need be, even to develope their principles to the utmost. And the Neri admit themselves to be wandering in a maze, without any fixed ideas of their own principles, and therefore are less frequently successful than the reverse; and they are equally obnoxious to the charge of departing farther from truth, than is necessary to give their own principles full play. Very recently a heresy of this faction adopted a peculiarity of tone, which is not to be found in the works of any of the great men of their party; and which is obnoxious to two serious objections. It is a greenish tone that unavoidably excites the idea of corruption and decay, which, having a tendency towards the disgusting, is not tolerable in the Fine Arts; and the second objection is, that, in their zeal for transparency, they had lost solidity to such an extent, that a portrait of George IV. by a celebrated artist, had the appearance of a vision, or of having been spun out of green glass bottles.

The beginner and the Amateur have already been warned against the dangers of green in pictures. And it may now be added, that transparency should reside in the *colours* to conceal the appearance of pigments, but that the substances represented should appear as *solid* as in nature.

CHAPTER III.

SECTION II.

COLOURS OF LIGHTS AND SHADOWS.

Whatever party of Colourists may find favour in the eyes of the reader, it will be necessary for him to be aware of certain effects observed in Nature, of which he will make such use as is admissible under the principle he may adopt.

Colours reside in the light parts of objects, if not brightest on the lightest parts, closely adjacent to them.

Shadows reduce, blacken, or render negative the colours of objects. The edges, extremities, or boundaries of *all* shadows are *grey*.

From the effect of contrast, shadows appear *comparatively* of the opposite colour to that of the light. The Bianchi take advantage of this circumstance, and sometimes force or increase the colour of the shadow, to bring out that of the light without really tinging it so *deeply* as is the case in Nature; whereby greater brilliancy is retained.

The colours of the lights and shadows depend upon that of the illuminating power, whether sunshine, moonlight, or grey daylight. These will be separately pointed out.

SUNSHINE

CHAPTER III.

SECTION III.

SUNSHINE.

The degree to which the colours of objects will be affected by that of the source of light, will very much depend upon the strength of the illuminating power.

The light of the noonday sun is so vivid that it diffuses its colour over all the illumined parts of the objects under its influence. These assume a rich golden hue, through which the local colours of the objects are slightly distinguishable, but rather as modifications of the warm tone diffused by the rays of the sun, than as integral varieties of tint.

As already has been noticed, the obvious effect of a yellowish light upon a blue object would be to induce a greenish tint; but in the case of sunshine, this is counteracted by the brilliancy of the light, and in representation, it is necessary for the same purpose, to infuse sufficient red into the light of blue objects under the influence of sunshine, or a disagreeable heavy effect will be produced.

Green, yellow, and orange objects become particularly brilliant in sunshine.

The shadows of the foreground are, in Nature, particularly negative or colourless; but as they recede, become gradually more blue. Sir Joshua Reynolds has made the shadows on the arm of his Sleeping Girl nearly black. He is one of the Neri. The Bianchi would have made them partake more of the colour opposite to that of light, purply brown, broken with red reflections. The shadows on green objects in the foreground would be rendered by dark crimson. Sir Thomas Lawrence frequently used pure lake in the shadows of his grass or shrubs. Plate.

CHAPTER III.

SECTION IV.

SUNSET.

At Sunset there is even less variety of colour observable in the illumined parts of objects than when the sun is higher in the sky. This arises from the influence of the atmosphere previously alluded to. A greater quantity of the medium is loaded with light, and the local colours of the objects seen through it are consequently affected to a greater degree thereby. The colour of the light is also affected by the medium through which it passes, and it becomes much richer, and more nearly approaching to orange.

The light in the sky, or illuminating power, is made yellow; but the lights on objects are rendered of a fleshy colour, which is made to appear warmer by the opposition of positive purple shadows, while those objects which do not receive any of the sun's light are kept very cool grey (the effect of reflected light from the blue sky), which by contrast throws the whole of the illuminated part of the picture into warmth. Frontispiece.

MOONLIGHT

CHAPTER III.

SECTION V.

MOONLIGHT.

The light of the moon being white or silvery grey, the shadows are made comparatively warm browns. The appearance of moonlight is given by the colours on the illuminated objects in the picture, which are made to appear cooler than they really are, by the contrast with the warm shadows. By this means, much more colour may be introduced into the light than is usually observed in Nature, and without impairing the effect of moonlight; and the Bianchi contend that by such means greater brilliancy is obtained. The blues in the sky near the moon are kept very pure for the same purpose. Plate.

GREY DAYLIGHT

CHAPTER III.

SECTION VI.

GREY DAYLIGHT.

Grey daylight also affords brownish shadows, but from the greater quantity and diffusion of comparatively colourless light, the local colours of objects become more visible, while the shadows are more varied by reflection and refraction. Reflections take their colours from those of the objects by which they are occasioned. The lights on objects are treated as in the case of moonlight; they are made *positively* warmer than they appear in nature, and are rendered *comparatively* cool by the warmth of the shadows.—Plate.

The degrees to which these licences may be carried, must depend upon the style of colouring adopted. The Amateur has had them placed before him, and whichever he may choose, he will be certain to meet with success in the eyes of one party; he cannot hope to please all.

9 783752 386035